JANE AUSTEN

Jane Austen was born in 1775 in Steventon, Hampshire, the daughter of an affluent village rector who encouraged her in her artistic pursuits. In 1801 she moved with her parents to Bath, but returned to Hampshire when her father died, settling in the village of Chawton. She remained there until 1817, when she moved to Winchester to be within easy reach of her doctor. She died that year, aged forty-one. Four of her novels, including *Pride and Prejudice*, were published anonymously in her lifetime; two more, along with several shorter works, appeared posthumously. She never married.

JANE AUSTEN

Jack and Alice

'Jack and Alice', 'Frederic and Elfrida', 'Henry and Eliza'
and 'The Three Sisters' first published 1933
'Evelyn' first published 1951

This edition first published 2026 by Macmillan Collector's Library
an imprint of Pan Macmillan
The Smithson, 6 Briset Street, London EC1M 5NR
EU representative: Macmillan Publishers Ireland Ltd, 1st Floor,
The Liffey Trust Centre, 117–126 Sheriff Street Upper,
Dublin 1 D01 YC43
Associated companies throughout the world

ISBN 978-1-0350-9865-1

1 3 5 7 9 8 6 4 2

A CIP catalogue record for this book is available from the British Library.

Cover design: Tiana-Jane Dunlop, Pan Macmillan Art Department
Typeset in Adobe Caslon Pro by Six Red Marbles UK, Thetford, Norfolk
Printed and bound in the UK using 100% Renewable Electricity by CPI Group (UK) Ltd

CONTENTS

Jack and Alice

1

Mr Johnson was once upon a time about fifty-three; in a twelvemonth afterwards he was fifty-four, which so much delighted him that he was determined to celebrate his next birthday by giving a masquerade to his children and friends. Accordingly, on the day he attained his fifty-fifth year tickets were dispatched to all his neighbours to that purpose. His acquaintance indeed in that part of the world were not very numerous as they consisted only of Lady Williams, Mr and Mrs Jones, Charles Adams and the three Miss Simpsons, who composed the neighbourhood of Pammydiddle and formed the masquerade.

Before I proceed to give an account of the evening, it will be proper to describe to my reader the persons and characters of the party introduced to his acquaintance.

Mr and Mrs Jones were both rather tall and very passionate, but were, in other respects, good-tempered, well-behaved people. Charles Adams was an amiable, accomplished and bewitching young man, of so dazzling a beauty that none but eagles could look him in the face. Miss Simpson was pleasing in her person, in her manners and in her disposition; an unbounded ambition was her only fault. Her second sister, Sukey, was envious, spiteful and malicious. Her person was short, fat and disagreeable. Cecilia (the youngest) was perfectly handsome but too affected to be pleasing. In Lady Williams every virtue met. She was a widow with a handsome jointure and the remains of a very handsome face. Though benevolent and candid, she was generous and sincere; though pious and good, she was religious and amiable; and though elegant and agreeable, she was polished and entertaining. The Johnsons were a family of love, and, though a little addicted to the bottle and the dice, had many good qualities.

Such was the party assembled in the elegant drawing-room of Johnson Court, among which the pleasing figure of a sultana was the most remarkable of the female masks. Of the males, a mask representing the sun, was the most universally admired. The beams that darted from his eyes were like those of that glorious luminary, though infinitely superior. So strong were they that no one dared venture within half a mile of them; he had therefore the best part of the room to himself, its size not amounting to more than three quarters of a mile in length and half a one in breadth. The gentleman at last finding the fierceness of his beams to be very inconvenient to the concourse by obliging them to crowd together in one corner of the room, half shut his eyes, by which means, the company discovered him to be Charles Adams in his plain green coat, without any mask at all.

When their astonishment was a little subsided their attention was attracted by two dominoes who advanced in a horrible passion; they were both very tall, but seemed in other respects to have many good qualities. 'These,' said the witty Charles, 'these are Mr and Mrs Jones,' and so indeed they were.

No one could imagine who was the sultana! Till at length, on her addressing a beautiful Flora, who was reclining in a studied attitude on a couch, with, 'Oh Cecilia, I wish I was really what I pretend to be,' she was discovered by the never failing genius of Charles Adams to be the elegant but ambitious Caroline Simpson, and the person to whom she addressed herself he rightly imagined to be her lovely but affected sister Cecilia.

The company now advanced to a gaming table where sat three dominoes (each with a bottle in their hand), deeply engaged; but a female in the character of Virtue fled with hasty footsteps from the shocking scene, while a little fat woman representing Envy, sat alternately at the elbows of the three gamesters. Charles Adams was still as bright as ever: he soon discovered the party at play to be the three Johnsons, Envy to be Sukey Simpson and Virtue to be Lady Williams.

The masks were then all removed and the company retired to another room to partake of an elegant and well-managed entertainment, after which the bottle being pretty briskly pushed about by the three Johnsons, the whole party not excepting even Virtue were carried home, dead drunk.

2

For three months did the masquerade afford ample subject for conversation to the inhabitants of Pammydiddle;

but no character at it was so fully expatiated on as Charles Adams. The singularity of his appearance, the beams which darted from his eyes, the brightness of his wit and the whole *tout ensemble* of his person had subdued the hearts of so many of the young ladies that of the six present at the masquerade but five had returned uncaptivated. Alice Johnson was the unhappy sixth, whose heart had not been able to withstand the power of his charms. But as it may appear strange to my readers that so much worth and excellence as he possessed should have conquered only hers, it will be necessary to inform them that the Miss Simpsons were defended from his power by ambition, envy and self-admiration. Every wish of Caroline was centred in a titled husband; while in Sukey such superior excellence could only raise her envy not her love; and Cecilia was too tenderly attached to herself to be pleased with anyone besides. As for Lady Williams and Mrs Jones, the former of them was too sensible to fall in love with one so much her junior and the latter, though very tall and very passionate, was too fond of her husband to think of such a thing.

Yet in spite of every endeavour on the part of Miss Johnson to discover any attachment to her in him, the cold and indifferent heart of Charles Adams still, to all appearance, preserved its native freedom; polite to all but partial to none, he still remained the lovely, the lively, but insensible Charles Adams.

One evening, Alice finding herself somewhat heated by wine (no very uncommon case), determined to seek a relief for her disordered head and love-sick heart in the conversation of the intelligent Lady Williams.

She found her ladyship at home, as was in general the case, for she was not fond of going out, and like the great Sir Charles Grandison, scorned to deny herself when at home, as she looked on that fashionable method of shutting out disagreeable visitors as little less than downright bigamy.

In spite of the wine she had been drinking, poor Alice was uncommonly out of spirits; she could think of nothing but Charles Adams, she could talk of nothing but him, and in short spoke so openly that Lady Williams soon discovered the unreturned affection she bore him, which excited her pity and compassion so strongly that she addressed her in the following manner.

'I perceive but too plainly, my dear Miss Johnson, that your heart has not been able to withstand the fascinating charms of this young man and I pity you sincerely. Is it a first love?'

'It is.'

'I am still more grieved to hear *that*; I am myself a sad example of the miseries in general attendant on a first love and I am determined for the future to avoid the like misfortune. I wish it may not be too late for you to do the same; if it is not, endeavour, my dear girl, to secure yourself from so great a danger. A second attachment is seldom attended with any serious consequences; against *that* therefore I have nothing to say. Preserve yourself from a first love and you need not fear a second.'

'You mentioned, madam, something of your having yourself been a sufferer by the misfortune you are so good as to wish me to avoid. Will you favour me with your life and adventures?'

'Willingly, my love.'

3

'My father was a gentleman of considerable fortune in Berkshire; myself and a few more, his only children. I was but six years old when I had the misfortune of losing my mother, and being at that time young and tender, my father, instead of sending me to school, procured an able-handed governess to superintend my education at home. My brothers were placed at schools suitable to their ages and my sisters, being all younger than myself, remained still under the care of their nurse.

'Miss Dickins was an excellent governess. She instructed me in the paths of virtue; under her tuition I daily became more amiable, and might perhaps by this time have nearly attained perfection, had not my worthy preceptoress been torn from my arms, e'er I had attained my seventeenth year. I never shall forget her last words. "My dear Kitty," she said, "goodnight t'ye." I never saw her afterwards,' continued Lady Williams, wiping her eyes. 'She eloped with the butler the same night.

'I was invited the following year by a distant relation of my father's to spend the winter with her in town. Mrs Watkins was a lady of fashion, family and fortune; she was in general esteemed a pretty woman, but I never thought her very handsome, for my part. She had too high a forehead, her eyes were too small and she had too much colour.'

'How can *that* be?' interrupted Miss Johnson, reddening with anger. 'Do you think that anyone can have too much colour?'

'Indeed I do, and I'll tell you why I do, my dear Alice; when a person has too great a degree of red in their complexion, it gives their face, in my opinion, too red a look.'

'But can a face, my lady, have too red a look?'

'Certainly, my dear Miss Johnson, and I'll tell you why. When a face has too red a look it does not appear to so much advantage as it would were it paler.'

'Pray, ma'am, proceed in your story.'

'Well, as I said before, I was invited by this lady to spend some weeks with her in town. Many gentlemen thought her handsome but, in my opinion, her forehead was too high, her eyes too small and she had too much colour.'

'In that, madam, as I said before, your ladyship must have been mistaken. Mrs Watkins could not have too much colour since no one can have too much.'

'Excuse me, my love, if I do not agree with you in that particular. Let me explain myself clearly; my idea of the case is this. When a woman has too great a proportion of red in her cheeks, she must have too much colour.'

'But, madam, I deny that it is possible for anyone to have too great a proportion of red in their cheeks.'

'What, my love, not if they have too much colour?'

Miss Johnson was now out of all patience, the more so perhaps as Lady Williams still remained so inflexibly cool. It must be remembered, however, that her ladyship had in one respect by far the advantage of Alice; I mean in not being drunk, for heated with wine and raised by passion she could have little command of her temper.

The dispute at length grew so hot on the part of Alice that 'from words she almost came to blows' – when Mr Johnson luckily entered and with some difficulty forced her away from Lady Williams, Mrs Watkins and her red cheeks.

4

My readers may perhaps imagine that after such a fracas, no intimacy could longer subsist between the Johnsons and Lady Williams, but in that they are mistaken, for her ladyship was too sensible to be angry at a conduct which she could not help perceiving to be the natural consequence of inebriety, and Alice had too sincere a respect for Lady Williams and too great a relish for her claret not to make every concession in her power.

A few days after their reconciliation, Lady Williams called on Miss Johnson to propose a walk in a citron grove which led from her ladyship's pigsty to Charles Adams's horse pond. Alice was too sensible of Lady Williams's kindness in proposing such a walk and too much pleased with the prospect of seeing, at the end of it, a horse pond of Charles's, not to accept it with visible delight.

They had not proceeded far before she was roused from the reflection of the happiness she was going to enjoy by Lady Williams's thus addressing her: 'I have as yet forborn, my dear Alice, to continue the narrative of my life from an unwillingness of recalling to your memory a scene which (since it reflects on you rather disgrace than credit) had better be forgot than remembered.'

Alice had already begun to colour up and was beginning to speak, when her ladyship, perceiving her displeasure, continued thus: 'I am afraid, my dear girl, that I have offended you by what I have just said; I assure you I do not mean to distress you by a retrospection of what cannot now be helped; considering all things, I do not think you so much to blame as many people do; for when a person is in liquor, there is no answering for what they may do; a woman in such a situation is particularly off her guard because her head is not strong enough to support intoxication.'

'Madam, this is not to be borne; I insist –'

'My dear girl, don't vex yourself about the matter; I assure you I have entirely forgiven everything respecting it; indeed, I was not angry at the time, because, as I saw all along, you were nearly dead drunk. I knew you could not help saying the strange things you did. But I see I distress you; so I will change the subject and desire it may never again be mentioned; remember it is all forgot – I will now pursue my story; but I must insist upon not giving you any description of Mrs Watkins: it would only be reviving old stories, and as you never saw her, it can be nothing to you if her forehead *was* too high, her eyes *were* too small, or if she *had* too much colour.'

'Again! Lady Williams: this is too much –' So provoked was poor Alice at this renewal of the old story that I know not what might have been the consequence of it had not their attention been engaged by another object. A lovely young woman, lying apparently in great pain beneath a citron tree, was an object too interesting not to attract their notice.

Forgetting their own dispute, they both with sympathising tenderness advanced towards her and accosted her in these terms: 'You seem, fair nymph, to be labouring under some misfortune which we shall be happy to relieve if you will inform us what it is. Will you favour us with your life and adventures?'

'Willingly, ladies, if you will be so kind as to be seated.' They took their places and she thus began.

5

'I am a native of North Wales and my father is one of the most capital tailors in it. Having a numerous family, he was easily prevailed on by a sister of my mother's, who is a widow in good circumstances and keeps an alehouse in the next village to ours, to let her take me and breed me up at her own expense. Accordingly, I have lived with her for the last eight years of my life, during which time she provided me with some of the first-rate masters, who taught me all the accomplishments requisite for one of my sex and rank. Under their instructions I learned dancing, music, drawing and various languages, by which means I became more accomplished than any other tailor's daughter in Wales. Never was there a happier creature than I was, till within the last half-year – but I should have told you before that the principal estate in our neighbourhood belongs to Charles Adams, the owner of the brick house you see yonder.'

'Charles Adams!' exclaimed the astonished Alice; 'are you acquainted with Charles Adams?'

'To my sorrow, madam, I am. He came about half a year ago to receive the rents of the estate I have just mentioned. At that time I first saw him; as you seem, ma'am, acquainted with him, I need not describe to you how charming he is. I could not resist his attractions –'

'Ah! who can,' said Alice with a deep sigh.

'My aunt, being in terms of the greatest intimacy with his cook, determined, at my request, to try whether she could discover, by means of her friend, if there were any chance of his returning my affection. For this purpose she went one evening to drink tea with Mrs Susan, who in the course of conversation mentioned the goodness of her place and the goodness of her master; upon which my aunt began pumping her with so much dexterity that in a short time Susan owned that she did not think her master would ever marry, "for," said she, "he has often and often declared to me that his wife, whoever she might be, must possess, youth, beauty, birth, wit, merit and money. I have many a time," she continued, "endeavoured to reason him out of his resolution and to convince him of the improbability of his ever meeting with such a lady; but my arguments have had no effect and he continues as firm in his determination as ever." You may imagine, ladies, my distress on hearing this; for I was fearful that though possessed of youth, beauty, wit and merit, and though the probable heiress of my aunt's house and business, he might think me deficient in rank, and, in being so, unworthy of his hand.

'However, I was determined to make a bold push and therefore wrote him a very kind letter, offering him with great tenderness my hand and heart. To this I received an angry and peremptory refusal, but thinking it might be rather the effect of his modesty than anything else, I pressed him again on the subject. But he never answered any more of my letters and very soon afterwards left the country. As soon as I heard of his departure I wrote to him here, informing him that I should shortly do myself the honour of waiting on him at Pammydiddle, to which I received no answer; therefore, choosing to take silence for consent, I left Wales, unknown to my aunt, and arrived here after a tedious journey this morning. On enquiring for his house, I was directed through this wood to the one you there see. With a heart elated by the expected happiness of beholding him, I entered the wood and had proceeded thus far in my progress through it, when I found myself suddenly seized by the leg, and on examining the cause of it, found that I was caught in one of the steel traps so common in gentlemen's grounds.'

'Ah!' cried Lady Williams, 'how fortunate we are to meet with you, since we might otherwise perhaps have shared the like misfortune.'

'It is indeed happy for you, ladies, that I should have been a short time before you. I screamed, as you may easily imagine, till the woods resounded again and till one of the inhuman wretch's servants came to my assistance and released me from my dreadful prison, but not before one of my legs was entirely broken.'

6

At this melancholy recital the fair eyes of Lady Williams were suffused in tears and Alice could not help exclaiming, 'Oh! cruel Charles, to wound the hearts and legs of all the fair.'

Lady Williams now interposed and observed that the young lady's leg ought to be set without further delay. After examining the fracture, therefore, she immediately began and performed the operation with great skill, which was the more wonderful on account of her having never performed such a one before. Lucy then arose from the ground, and finding that she could walk with the greatest ease, accompanied them to Lady Williams's house at her ladyship's particular request.

The perfect form, the beautiful face and elegant manners of Lucy so won on the affections of Alice that when they parted, which was not till after supper, she assured her that, except her father, brother, uncles, aunts, cousins and other relations, Lady Williams, Charles Adams and a few dozen more of particular friends, she loved her better than almost any other person in the world.

Such a flattering assurance of her regard would justly have given much pleasure to the object of it, had she not plainly perceived that the amiable Alice had partaken too freely of Lady Williams's claret.

Her ladyship (whose discernment was great) read in the intelligent countenance of Lucy her thoughts on the subject, and as soon as Miss Johnson had taken her leave, thus addressed her: 'When you are more intimately acquainted with my Alice you will not be surprised, Lucy, to see the dear creature drink a little too much; for such things happen every day. She has many rare and charming qualities, but sobriety is not one of them. The whole family are indeed a sad drunken set. I am sorry to say too that I never knew three such thorough gamesters as they are, more particularly Alice. But she is a charming girl. I fancy not one of the sweetest tempers in the world – to be sure, I have seen her in such passions! However, she is a sweet young woman. I am sure you'll like her. I scarcely know anyone so amiable. Oh! that you could but have seen her the other evening! How she raved! And on such a trifle too! She is indeed a most pleasing girl! I shall always love her!'

'She appears by your ladyship's account to have many good qualities,' replied Lucy.

'Oh! a thousand,' answered Lady Williams; 'though I am very partial to her, and perhaps am blinded by my affection to her real defects.'

7

The next morning brought the three Miss Simpsons to wait on Lady Williams, who received them with the utmost politeness and introduced to their acquaintance Lucy, with whom the eldest was so much pleased that at parting she declared her sole ambition was to have her accompany them the next morning to Bath, whither they were going for some weeks.

'Lucy,' said Lady Williams, 'is quite at her own disposal, and if she chooses to accept so kind an invitation, I hope she will not hesitate from any motives of delicacy on my account. I know not, indeed, how I shall ever be able to part with her. She never was at Bath and I should think that it would be a most agreeable jaunt to her. Speak, my love,' continued she, turning to Lucy, 'what say you to accompanying these ladies? I shall be miserable without you – 'twill be a most pleasant tour to you – I hope you'll go; if you do, I am sure 'twill be the death of me – pray be persuaded.'

Lucy begged leave to decline the honour of accompanying them, with many expressions of gratitude for the extreme politeness of Miss Simpson in inviting her.

Miss Simpson appeared much disappointed by her refusal. Lady Williams insisted on her going – declared that she would never forgive her if she did not, and that she should never survive it if she did, in short used such persuasive arguments that it was at length resolved she was to go. The Miss Simpsons called for her at ten o'clock the next morning and Lady Williams had soon the satisfaction of receiving from her young friend the pleasing intelligence of their safe arrival in Bath.

It may now be proper to return to the hero of this novel, Jack the brother of Alice, of whom I believe I have scarcely ever had occasion to speak; which may perhaps be partly owing to his unfortunate propensity to liquor, which so completely deprived him of the use of those faculties nature had endowed him with that he never did anything worth mentioning. His death happened a short time after Lucy's departure and was the natural consequence of this pernicious practice. By his decease, his sister became the sole inheritress of a very large fortune, which, as it gave her fresh hopes of rendering herself acceptable as a wife to Charles Adams, could not fail of being most pleasing to her – and as the effect was joyful the cause could scarcely be lamented.

Finding the violence of her attachment to him daily augment, she at length disclosed it to her father and desired him to propose a union between them to Charles. Her father consented and set out one morning to open the affair to the young man. Mr Johnson being a man of few words, his part was soon performed and the answer he received was as follows.

'Sir, I may perhaps be expected to appear pleased at and grateful for the offer you have made me: but let me tell you that I consider it as an affront. I look upon myself to be, sir, a perfect beauty – where would you see a finer figure or a more charming face? Then, sir, I imagine my manners and address to be of the most polished kind; there is a certain elegance, a peculiar sweetness in them that I never saw equalled and cannot describe. Partiality aside, I am certainly more accomplished in every language, every science, every art and everything than any other person in Europe. My temper is even, my virtues innumerable, my self unparalleled. Since such, sir, is my character, what do you mean by wishing me to marry your daughter? Let me give you a short sketch of yourself and of her. I look upon you, sir, to be a very good sort of man in the main; a drunken old dog to be sure, but that's nothing to me. Your daughter, sir, is neither sufficiently beautiful, sufficiently amiable, sufficiently witty, nor sufficiently rich for me. I expect nothing more in my wife than my wife will find in me – perfection. These, sir, are my sentiments and I honour myself for having such. One friend I have and glory in having but one. She is at present preparing my dinner, but if you choose to see her, she shall come and she will inform you that these have ever been my sentiments.'

Mr Johnson was satisfied, and, expressing himself to be much obliged to Mr Adams for the characters he had favoured him with of himself and his daughter, took his leave.

The unfortunate Alice, on receiving from her father the sad account of the ill success his visit had been attended with, could scarcely support the disappointment. She flew to her bottle and it was soon forgot.

8

While these affairs were transacting at Pammydiddle, Lucy was conquering every heart at Bath. A fortnight's residence there had nearly effaced from her remembrance the captivating form of Charles. The recollection of what her heart had formerly suffered by his charms and her leg by his trap enabled her to forget him with tolerable ease, which was what she determined to do; and for that purpose dedicated five minutes in every day to the employment of driving him from her remembrance.

Her second letter to Lady Williams contained the pleasing intelligence of her having accomplished her undertaking to her entire satisfaction; she mentioned in it also an offer of marriage she had received from the Duke of — , an elderly man of noble fortune whose ill health was the chief inducement of his journey to Bath.

> I am distressed [she continued] to know whether I mean to accept him or not. There are a thousand advantages to be derived from a marriage with the duke, for besides those more inferior ones of rank and fortune it will procure me a home, which of all other things is what I most desire. Your ladyship's kind wish of my always remaining with you is noble and generous, but I cannot think of becoming so great a burden on one I so much love and esteem. That one should receive obligations only from those we despise is a sentiment instilled into my mind by my worthy aunt, in my early years, and cannot in my opinion be too strictly adhered to. The excellent woman of whom I now speak is, I hear, too much incensed by my imprudent departure from Wales to receive me again. I most earnestly wish to leave the ladies I am now with. Miss Simpson is indeed (setting aside ambition) very amiable, but her second sister, the envious and malevolent Sukey, is too disagreeable to live with. I have reason to think that the admiration I have met with in the circles of the great at this place has raised her hatred and envy; for often has she threatened and sometimes endeavoured to cut my throat. Your ladyship will therefore allow that I am not wrong in wishing to leave Bath, and in wishing to have a home to receive me, when I do. I

shall expect with impatience your advice concerning the duke and am your most obliged

LUCY

Lady Williams sent her her opinion on the subject in the following manner:

Why do you hesitate, my dearest Lucy, a moment with respect to the duke? I have enquired into his character and find him to be an unprincipled, illiterate man. Never shall my Lucy be united to such a one! He has a princely fortune, which is every day increasing. How nobly will you spend it! what credit will you give him in the eyes of all! How much will he be respected on his wife's account! But why, my dearest Lucy, why will you not at once decide this affair by returning to me and never leaving me again? Although I admire your noble sentiments with respect to obligations, yet let me beg that they may not prevent your making me happy. It will, to be sure, be a great expense to me to have you always with me – I shall not be able to support it – but what is that in comparison with the happiness I shall enjoy in your society? 'Twill ruin me, I know – you will not therefore, surely, withstand these arguments, or refuse to return to yours most affectionately,

C. WILLIAMS

9

What might have been the effect of her ladyship's advice had it ever been received by Lucy is uncertain as it reached Bath a few hours after she had breathed her last. She fell a sacrifice to the envy and malice of Sukey, who, jealous of her superior charms, took her by poison from an admiring world at the age of seventeen.

Thus fell the amiable and lovely Lucy, whose life had been marked by no crime and stained by no blemish but her imprudent departure from her aunt's, and whose death was sincerely lamented by everyone who knew her. Among the most afflicted of her friends were Lady Williams, Miss Johnson and the duke, the two first of whom had a most sincere regard for her, more particularly Alice, who had spent a whole evening in her company and had never thought of her since. His grace's affliction may likewise be easily accounted for, since he lost one for whom he had experienced, during the last ten days, a tender affection and sincere regard. He mourned her loss with unshaken constancy for the next fortnight, at the end of which time he gratified the ambition of Caroline Simpson by raising her to the rank of a duchess. Thus was she at length rendered completely happy in the gratification of her favourite passion. Her sister, the perfidious Sukey, was likewise shortly after exalted in a manner she truly deserved, and by her actions appeared to have always desired. Her barbarous murder was discovered and in spite of every interceding friend she was speedily raised to the gallows. The beautiful but affected Cecilia was too sensible of her own superior charms not to imagine that if Caroline could engage a duke she might without censure aspire to the affections of some prince – and knowing that those of her native country were chiefly engaged, she left England, and I have since heard is at present the favourite sultana of the Great Mogul.

In the meantime, the inhabitants of Pammydiddle were in a state of the greatest astonishment and wonder, a report being circulated of the intended marriage of Charles Adams. The lady's name was still a secret. Mr and Mrs Jones imagined it to be Miss Johnson, but *she* knew better; all *her* fears were centred in his cook, when, to the astonishment of everyone, he was publicly united to Lady Williams.

Frederic and Elfrida

1

The uncle of Elfrida was the father of Frederic; in other words, they were first cousins by the father's side.

Being both born in one day and both brought up at one school, it was not wonderful that they should look on each other with something more than bare politeness. They loved with mutual sincerity but were both determined not to transgress the rules of propriety by owning their attachment, either to the object beloved or to anyone else.

They were exceedingly handsome and so much alike that it was not everyone who knew them apart. Nay, even their most intimate friends had nothing to distinguish them by but the shape of the face, the colour of the eye, the length of the nose and the difference of the complexion.

Elfrida had an intimate friend to whom, being on a visit to an aunt, she wrote the following letter:

To Miss Drummond

DEAR CHARLOTTE – I should be obliged to you if you would buy me, during your stay with

Mrs Williamson, a new and fashionable bonnet to suit the complexion of your
E. FALKNOR

Charlotte, whose character was a willingness to oblige everyone, when she returned into the country brought her friend the wished-for bonnet, and so ended this little adventure, much to the satisfaction of all parties.

On her return to Crankhumdunberry (of which sweet village her father was rector), Charlotte was received with the greatest joy by Frederic and Elfrida, who, after pressing her alternately to their bosoms, proposed to her to take a walk in a grove of poplars which led from the parsonage to a verdant lawn enamelled with a variety of variegated flowers and watered by a purling stream, brought from the Valley of Tempe by a passage underground.

In this grove they had scarcely remained above nine hours, when they were suddenly agreeably surprised by hearing a most delightful voice warble the following stanza.

SONG

'That Damon was in love with me
I once thought and believ'd,
But now that he is not I see,
I fear I was deceiv'd.'

No sooner were the lines finished than they beheld by a turning in the grove two elegant young women leaning on each other's arms, who, immediately on perceiving them, took a different path and disappeared from their sight.

2

As Elfrida and her companions had seen enough of them to know that they were neither the two Miss Greens nor Mrs Jackson and her daughter, they could not help expressing their surprise at their appearance, till at length, recollecting that a new family had lately taken a house not far from the grove, they hastened home, determined to lose no time in forming an acquaintance with two such amiable and worthy girls, of which family they rightly imagined them to be a part.

Agreeable to such a determination, they went that very evening to pay their respects to Mrs Fitzroy and her two daughters. On being shown into an elegant dressing-room, ornamented with festoons of artificial flowers, they were struck with the engaging exterior and beautiful outside of Jezalinda, the elder of the young ladies; but e'er they had been many minutes seated, the wit and charms which shone resplendent in the conversation of the amiable Rebecca enchanted them so much that they all with one accord jumped up and exclaimed: 'Lovely and too charming fair one, notwithstanding your forbidding squint, your greasy tresses and your swelling back, which are more frightful than imagination can paint or pen describe, I cannot refrain from expressing my raptures, at the engaging qualities of your mind, which so amply atone for the horror with which your first appearance must ever inspire the unwary visitor.

'Your sentiments so nobly expressed on the different excellencies of Indian and English muslins, and the judicious preference you give the former, have excited in me an admiration of which I can alone give an adequate idea by assuring you it is nearly equal to what I feel for myself.'

Then making a profound curtsey to the amiable and abashed Rebecca, they left the room and hurried home.

From this period, the intimacy between the families of Fitzroy, Drummond and Falknor daily increased till at length it grew to such a pitch that they did not scruple to kick one another out of the window on the slightest provocation.

During this happy state of harmony, the elder Miss Fitzroy ran off with the coachman and the amiable Rebecca was asked in marriage by Captain Roger of Buckinghamshire.

Mrs Fitzroy did not approve of the match on account of the tender years of the young couple, Rebecca being but thirty-six and Captain Roger little more than sixty-three. To remedy this objection, it was agreed that they should wait a little while till they were a good deal older.

3

In the meantime, the parents of Frederic proposed to those of Elfrida a union between them, which being accepted with pleasure, the wedding clothes were bought and nothing remained to be settled but the naming of the day.

As to the lovely Charlotte, being importuned with eagerness to pay another visit to her aunt, she determined to accept the invitation and in consequence of it walked to Mrs Fitzroy's to take leave of the amiable Rebecca, whom she found surrounded by patches, powder, pomatum and paint with which she was vainly endeavouring to remedy the natural plainness of her face.

'I am come, my amiable Rebecca, to take my leave of you for the fortnight I am destined to spend with my aunt. Believe me, this separation is painful to me, but it is as necessary as the labour which now engages you.'

'Why, to tell you the truth, my love,' replied Rebecca, 'I have lately taken it into my head to think (perhaps with little reason) that my complexion is by no means equal to the rest of my face and have therefore taken, as you see, to white and red paint, which I would scorn to use on any other occasion as I hate art.'

Charlotte, who perfectly understood the meaning of her friend's speech, was too good-tempered and obliging to refuse her what she knew she wished – a compliment; and they parted the best friends in the world.

With a heavy heart and streaming eyes did she ascend the lovely vehicle – a post-chaise – which bore her from her friends and home; but grieved as she was, she little thought in what a strange and different manner she should return to it.

On her entrance into the city of London, which

was the place of Mrs Williamson's abode, the postilion, whose stupidity was amazing, declared – and declared even without the least shame or compunction – that having never been informed, he was totally ignorant of what part of the town he was to drive to.

Charlotte, whose nature we have before intimated was an earnest desire to oblige everyone, with the greatest condescension and good-humour informed him that he was to drive to Portland Place, which he accordingly did, and Charlotte soon found herself in the arms of a fond aunt.

Scarcely were they seated – as usual, in the most affectionate manner in one chair – than the door suddenly opened and an aged gentleman with a sallow face and old pink coat, partly by intention and partly through weakness, was at the feet of the lovely Charlotte, declaring his attachment to her and beseeching her pity in the most moving manner.

Not being able to resolve to make anyone miserable, she consented to become his wife; whereupon the gentleman left the room and all was quiet.

Their quiet, however, continued but a short time, for on a second opening of the door, a young and handsome gentleman with a new blue coat entered and entreated from the lovely Charlotte permission to pay to her his addresses.

There was a something in the appearance of the second stranger that influenced Charlotte in his favour, to the full as much as the appearance of the first: she could not account for it, but so it was.

Having therefore, agreeable to that natural turn of her mind to make everyone happy, promised to become his wife the next morning, he took his leave and the two ladies sat down to supper on a young leveret, a brace of partridges, a leash of pheasants and a dozen of pigeons.

4

It was not till the next morning that Charlotte recollected the double engagement she had entered into; but when she did, the reflection of her past folly operated so strongly on her mind that she resolved to be guilty of a greater, and to that end threw herself into a deep stream which ran through her aunt's pleasure grounds in Portland Place.

She floated to Crankhumdunberry where she was picked up and buried; the following epitaph, composed by Frederic, Elfrida and Rebecca, was placed on her tomb:

EPITAPH

Here lies our friend who, having promised
That unto two she would be married,
Threw her sweet body and her lovely face
Into the stream that runs through Portland Place.

These sweet lines, as pathetic as beautiful, were never read by anyone who passed that way without a shower of tears, which if they should fail of exciting in you, reader, your mind must be unworthy to peruse them.

Having performed the last sad office to their departed friend, Frederic and Elfrida, together with Captain Roger and Rebecca, returned to Mrs Fitzroy's, at whose feet they threw themselves with one accord and addressed her in the following manner.

'Madam, when the sweet Captain Roger first addressed the amiable Rebecca, you alone objected to their union on account of the tender years of the parties. That plea can be no more, seven days being now expired, together with the lovely Charlotte, since the captain first spoke to you on the subject.

'Consent then, madam, to their union, and as a reward, this smelling bottle which I enclose in my right hand shall be yours and yours for ever; I never will claim it again. But if you refuse to join their hands in three days' time, this dagger which I enclose in my left shall be steeped in your heart's blood.

'Speak then, madam, and decide their fate and yours.'

Such gentle and sweet persuasion could not fail of having the desired effect. The answer they received was this. 'My dear young friends, the arguments you have used are too just and too eloquent to be withstood; Rebecca, in three days' time, you shall be united to the captain.'

This speech, than which nothing could be more satisfactory, was received with joy by all; and peace being once more restored on all sides, Captain Roger entreated Rebecca to favour them with a song, in compliance with which request, having first assured them that she had a terrible cold, she sang as follows:

SONG

'When Corydon went to the fair
He bought a red ribbon for Bess,
With which she encircled her hair
And made herself look very fess.'

5

At the end of three days, Captain Roger and Rebecca were united and immediately after the ceremony set off in the stage-waggon for the captain's seat in Buckinghamshire.

The parents of Elfrida, although they earnestly wished to see her married to Frederic before they died, yet, knowing the delicate frame of her mind could ill bear the least exertion and rightly judging that naming her wedding day would be too great a one, forbore to press her on the subject.

Weeks and fortnights flew away without gaining the least ground; the clothes grew out of fashion and at length Captain Roger and his lady arrived to pay a visit to their mother and introduce to her their beautiful daughter of eighteen.

Elfrida, who had found her former acquaintance were growing too old and too ugly to be any longer agreeable, was rejoiced to hear of the arrival of so pretty a girl as Eleanor, with whom she determined to form the strictest friendship.

But the happiness she had expected from an

acquaintance with Eleanor she soon found was not to be received, for she had not only the mortification of finding herself treated by her as little less than an old woman, but had actually the horror of perceiving a growing passion in the bosom of Frederic for the daughter of the amiable Rebecca.

The instant she had the first idea of such an attachment, she flew to Frederic and, in a manner truly heroic, spluttered out to him her intention of being married the next day.

To one in his predicament who possessed less personal courage than Frederic was master of, such a speech would have been death; but he, not being the least terrified, boldly replied, 'Damme, Elfrida, *you* may be married tomorrow but *I* won't.'

This answer distressed her too much for her delicate constitution. She accordingly fainted, and was in such a hurry to have a succession of fainting fits that she had scarcely patience enough to recover from one before she fell into another.

Though in any threatening danger to his life or liberty, Frederic was as bold as brass, yet in other respects his heart was as soft as cotton, and immediately on hearing of the dangerous way Elfrida was in, he flew to her, and finding her better than he had been taught to expect, was united to her for ever.

Henry and Eliza

As Sir George and Lady Harcourt were superintending the labours of their haymakers, rewarding the industry of some by smiles of approbation and punishing the idleness of others by a cudgel, they perceived, lying closely concealed beneath the thick foliage of a haycock, a beautiful little girl not more than three months old.

Touched with the enchanting graces of her face and delighted with the infantine though sprightly answers she returned to their many questions, they resolved to take her home and, having no children of their own, to educate her with care and cost.

Being good people themselves, their first and principal care was to incite in her a love of virtue and a hatred of vice, in which they so well succeeded (Eliza having a natural turn that way herself) that when she grew up, she was the delight of all who knew her.

Beloved by Lady Harcourt, adored by Sir George and admired by all the world, she lived in a continued course of uninterrupted happiness till she had attained her eighteenth year, when, happening one day to be detected in stealing a banknote of £50, she was turned out of doors by her inhuman benefactors. Such a transition to one who did not possess so noble and exalted a mind as Eliza would have been death, but she, happy in the conscious knowledge of her own excellence, amused herself, as she sat beneath a tree, with making and singing the following lines:

'Though misfortune my footsteps may ever attend,
I hope I shall never have need of a friend,
as an innocent heart I will ever preserve
and will never from virtue's dear boundaries swerve.'

Having amused herself some hours with this song and her own pleasing reflections, she arose and took the road to M—, a small market town of which place her most intimate friend kept the Red Lion.

To this friend she immediately went, and having recounted her late misfortune, she communicated her wish of getting into some family in the capacity of humble companion.

Mrs Wilson, who was the most amiable creature on earth, was no sooner acquainted with her desire than she sat down in the bar and wrote the following letter to the Duchess of F—, the woman whom of all others she most esteemed.

To the Duchess of F—

Receive into your family, at my request, a young woman of unexceptionable character, who is so good as to choose your society in preference to going to service. Hasten, and take her from the arms of your
SARAH WILSON

The duchess, whose friendship for Mrs Wilson would have carried her any lengths, was overjoyed at such an opportunity of obliging her, and accordingly set out immediately on the receipt of her letter for the Red Lion, which she reached the same evening. The Duchess of F— was about forty-five and a half; her passions were strong, her friendships firm and her enmities unconquerable. She was a widow and had only one daughter, who was on the point of marriage with a young man of considerable fortune.

The duchess no sooner beheld our heroine than, throwing her arms around her neck, she declared herself so much pleased with her that she was resolved they never more should part. Eliza was delighted with such a protestation of friendship, and after taking a most affecting leave of her dear Mrs Wilson, accompanied her grace the next morning to her seat in Surrey.

With every expression of regard did the duchess introduce her to Lady Harriet, who was so much pleased with Eliza's appearance that she besought her to consider her as her sister, which Eliza with the greatest condescension promised to do.

Mr Cecil, the lover of Lady Harriet, being often with the family was often with Eliza. A mutual love took place, and Cecil, having declared his first, prevailed on Eliza to consent to a private union, which was easy to be effected as the duchess's chaplain, being very much in love with Eliza himself, would, they were certain, do anything to oblige her.

The duchess and Lady Harriet being engaged one evening to an assembly, they took the opportunity of their absence and were united by the enamoured chaplain.

When the ladies returned, their amazement was great at finding instead of Eliza the following note:

MADAM – We are married and gone.
HENRY AND ELIZA CECIL

Her grace as soon as she had read the letter, which sufficiently explained the whole affair, flew into the most violent passion, and after having spent an agreeable half-hour in calling them by all the shocking names her rage could suggest to her, sent out after them three hundred armed men, with orders not to return without their bodies, dead or alive; intending if they should be brought to her in the latter condition to have them put to death in some torturelike manner after a few years' confinement.

In the meantime, Cecil and Eliza continued their flight to the continent, which they judged to be more secure than their native land from the dreadful effects of the duchess's vengeance, which they had so much reason to apprehend.

In France they remained three years, during which time they became the parents of two boys, and at the end of it Eliza became a widow without anything to support either her or her children. They had lived since their marriage at the rate of £18,000 a year, of which Mr Cecil's estate being rather less than the twentieth part, they had been able to save but a trifle, having lived to the utmost extent of their income.

Eliza, being perfectly conscious of the derangement in their affairs, immediately on her husband's death set sail for England, in a man-of-war of fifty-five guns, which they had had built in their more prosperous days. But no sooner had she stepped on shore at Dover, with a child in each hand, than she was seized by the officers of the duchess, and conducted by them to a snug little Newgate of their lady's, which she had erected for the reception of her own private prisoners.

No sooner had Eliza entered her dungeon than the first thought which occurred to her was how to get out of it again. She went to the door, but it was locked. She looked at the window, but it was barred with iron. Disappointed in both her expectations, she despaired of effecting her escape, when she fortunately perceived in a corner of her cell a small saw and ladder of ropes. With the saw she instantly went to work and in a few weeks had displaced every bar but one, to which she fastened the ladder.

A difficulty then occurred which for some time she knew not how to obviate. Her children were too small to get down the ladder by themselves, nor would it be possible for her to take them in her arms when *she* made the descent. At last she determined to fling down all her clothes, of which she had a large quantity, and then, having given them strict charge not to hurt themselves, throw her children after them. She herself with ease descended by the ladder, at the bottom of which she had the pleasure of finding her little boys in perfect health and fast asleep.

Her wardrobe she now saw a fatal necessity of selling,

both for the preservation of her children and herself. With tears in her eyes, she parted with these last relics of her former glory, and with the money she got for them, bought others more useful, some playthings for her boys and a gold watch for herself.

But scarcely was she provided with the above-mentioned necessaries than she began to find herself rather hungry, and had reason to think, by their biting off two of her fingers, that her children were much in the same situation.

To remedy these unavoidable misfortunes, she determined to return to her old friends, Sir George and Lady Harcourt, whose generosity she had so often experienced and hoped to experience as often again.

She had about forty miles to travel before she could reach their hospitable mansion; having walked thirty without stopping, she found herself at the entrance of a town where often in happier times she had accompanied Sir George and Lady Harcourt to there regale themselves with a cold collation at one of the inns.

The reflections that her adventures since the last time she had partaken of these happy junketings afforded her occupied her mind for some time as she sat on the steps at the door of a gentleman's house. As soon as these reflections were ended, she arose and determined to take her station at the very inn she remembered with so much delight, from the company of which, as they went in and out, she hoped to receive some charitable gratuity.

She had but just taken her post at the inn-yard before a carriage drove out of it, and on turning the corner at which she was stationed, stopped to give the postilion an opportunity of admiring the beauty of the prospect. Eliza then advanced to the carriage, and was going to request their charity, when, on fixing her eyes on the lady within it, she exclaimed, 'Lady Harcourt!'

To which the lady replied, 'Eliza!'

'Yes, madam, it is the wretched Eliza herself.'

Sir George, who was also in the carriage, but too much amazed to speak, was proceeding to demand an explanation from Eliza of the situation she was then in, when Lady Harcourt, in transports of joy, exclaimed, 'Sir George, Sir George, she is not only Eliza our adopted daughter, but our real child.'

'Our real child! What, Lady Harcourt, do you mean? You know you never even were with child. Explain yourself, I beseech you.'

'You must remember, Sir George, that when you sailed for America, you left me breeding.'

'I do, I do. Go on, dear Polly.'

'Four months after you were gone, I was delivered of this girl, but dreading your just resentment at her not proving the boy you wished, I took her to a haycock and laid her down. A few weeks afterwards, you returned, and, fortunately for me, made no enquiries on the subject. Satisfied within myself of the welfare of my child, I soon forgot I had one, insomuch that when we shortly after found her in the very haycock I had placed her, I had no more idea of her being my own than you had, and nothing, I will venture to say, would have recalled the circumstance to my remembrance but my thus accidentally hearing her voice, which now strikes me as being the very counterpart of my own child's.'

'The rational and convincing account you have given of the whole affair,' said Sir George, 'leaves no doubt of her being our daughter and as such I freely forgive the robbery she was guilty of.'

A mutual reconciliation then took place, and Eliza, ascending the carriage with her two children, returned to that home from which she had been absent nearly four years.

No sooner was she reinstated in her accustomed power at Harcourt Hall than she raised an army with which she entirely demolished the duchess's Newgate, snug as it was, and by that act gained the blessings of thousands and the applause of her own heart.

The Three Sisters

1

MISS STANHOPE TO MRS —

MY DEAR FANNY – I am the happiest creature in the world, for I have received an offer of marriage from Mr Watts. It is the first I have ever had and I hardly know how to value it enough. How I will triumph over the Duttons! I do not intend to accept it, at least I believe not, but as I am not quite certain I gave him an equivocal answer and left him. And now, my dear Fanny, I want your advice whether I should accept his offer or not, and that you may be able to judge of his merits and the situation of affairs I will give you an account of them. He is quite an old man, about two-and-thirty, very plain, *so* plain that I cannot bear to look at him. He is extremely disagreeable and I hate him more than anybody else in the world. He has a large fortune and will make great settlements on me; but then he is very healthy. In short, I do not know what to do. If I refuse him he as good as told me that he should offer himself to Sophia and if *she* refused him to Georgiana, and I could not bear to have either of them married before me. If I accept him I know I shall be miserable all the rest of my life, for he is very ill tempered and peevish, extremely jealous, and so stingy that there is no living in the house with him. He told me he should mention the affair to mama, but I insisted upon it that he did not, for very likely she would make me marry him whether I would or no; however, probably he *has* before now, for he never does anything he is desired to do. I believe I shall have him. It will be such a triumph to be married before Sophy, Georgiana and the Duttons. And he promised to have a new carriage on the occasion, but we almost quarrelled about the colour, for I insisted upon its being blue spotted with silver, and he declared it should be a plain chocolate; and to provoke me more, said it should be just as low as his old one. I won't have him, I declare. He said he should come again tomorrow and take my final answer, so I believe I must get him while I can. I know the Duttons will envy me and I shall be able to chaperone Sophy and Georgiana to all the winter balls. But then what will be the use of that when very likely he won't let me go myself, for I know he hates dancing, and what he hates himself he has no idea of any other person's liking; and, besides, he talks a great deal of women always staying at home and such stuff. I believe I shan't have him; I would refuse him at once if I were certain that neither of my sisters would accept him, and that if they did not, he would not offer to the Duttons. I cannot run such a risk, so, if he will promise to have the carriage ordered as I like, I will have him, if not he may ride in it by himself for me. I hope you like my determination; I can think of nothing better.

And am your ever affectionate
MARY STANHOPE

2

DEAR FANNY – I had but just sealed my last letter to you when my mother came up and told me she wanted to speak to me on a very particular subject.

'Ah! I know what you mean,' said I; 'that old fool Mr Watts has told you all about it, though I bid him not. However, you shan't force me to have him if I don't like it.'

'I am not going to force you, child, but only want to know what your resolution is with regard to his proposals, and to insist upon your making up your mind one way or t'other so that if *you* don't accept him *Sophy* may.'

'Indeed,' replied I hastily, 'Sophy need not trouble herself for I shall certainly marry him myself.'

'If that is your resolution,' said my mother, 'why should you be afraid of my forcing your inclinations?'

'Why, because I have not settled whether I shall have him or not.'

'You are the strangest girl in the world, Mary. What you say one moment, you unsay the next. Do tell me, once for all, whether you intend to marry Mr Watts or not?'

'Lor, mama, how can I tell you what I don't know myself?'

'Then I desire you will know, and quickly too, for Mr Watts says he won't be kept in suspense.'

'That depends upon me.'

'No, it does not, for if you do not give him your final answer tomorrow when he drinks tea with us, he intends to pay his addresses to Sophy.'

'Then I shall tell all the world that he behaved very ill to me.'

'What good will that do? Mr Watts has been too long abused by all the world to mind it now.'

'I wish I had a father or a brother because then they should fight him.'

'They would be cunning if they did, for Mr Watts would run away first; and therefore you must and shall resolve either to accept or refuse him before tomorrow evening.'

'But why, if I don't have him, must he offer to my sisters?'

'Why! because he wishes to be allied to the family and because they are as pretty as you are.'

'But will Sophy marry him, mama, if he offers to her?'

'Most likely. Why should not she? If, however, she does not choose it, then Georgiana must, for I am determined not to let such an opportunity escape of settling one of my daughters so advantageously. So, make the most of your time; I leave you to settle the matter with yourself.'

And then she went away. The only thing I

can think of, my dear Fanny, is to ask Sophy and Georgiana whether they would have him were he to make proposals to them, and if they say they would not I am resolved to refuse him too, for I hate him more than you can imagine. As for the Duttons, if he marries one of *them* I shall still have the triumph of having refused him first. So, adieu, my dear friend –

Yours ever,

M. S.

3

MISS GEORGIANA STANHOPE TO MISS —

Wednesday

MY DEAR ANNE – Sophy and I have just been practising a little deceit on our eldest sister, to which we are not perfectly reconciled, and yet the circumstances were such that if anything will excuse it, they must. Our neighbour Mr Watts has made proposals to Mary: proposals which she knew not how to receive, for though she has a particular dislike to him (in which she is not singular) yet she would willingly marry him sooner than risk his offering to Sophy or me, which, in case of a refusal from herself, he told her he should do, for you must know the poor girl considers our marrying before her as one of the greatest misfortunes that can possibly befall her, and to prevent it would willingly ensure herself everlasting misery by a marriage with Mr Watts. An hour ago she came to us to sound our inclinations respecting the affair, which were to determine hers.

A little before she came my mother had given us an account of it, telling us that she certainly would not let him go farther than our own family for a wife. 'And therefore,' said she, 'if Mary won't have him, Sophy must, and if Sophy won't, Georgiana *shall*.' Poor Georgiana! We neither of us attempted to alter my mother's resolution, which I am sorry to say is generally more strictly kept than rationally formed. As soon as she was gone, however, I broke silence to assure Sophy that if Mary should refuse Mr Watts, I should not expect her to sacrifice *her* happiness by becoming his wife from a motive of generosity to me, which I was afraid her good nature and sisterly affection might induce her to do.

'Let us flatter ourselves,' replied she, 'that Mary will not refuse him. Yet how can I hope that my sister may accept a man who cannot make her happy.'

'*He* cannot, it is true, but his fortune, his name, his house, his carriage will, and I have no doubt but that Mary will marry him; indeed, why should she not? He is not more than two-and-thirty, a very proper age for a man to marry at. He is rather plain, to be sure, but then what is beauty in a man? If he has but a genteel figure and a sensible-looking face it is quite sufficient.'

'This is all very true, Georgiana, but Mr Watts's figure is unfortunately extremely vulgar and his countenance is very heavy.'

'And then as to his temper: it has been reckoned bad, but may not the world be deceived in their judgement of it? There is an open frankness in his disposition which becomes a man. They say he is stingy; we'll call that prudence. They say he is suspicious. *That* proceeds from a warmth of heart always excusable in youth, and in short I see no reason why he should not make a very good husband, or why Mary should not be very happy with him.'

Sophy laughed; I continued, 'However, whether Mary accepts him or not I am resolved. My determination is made. I never would marry Mr Watts were beggary the only alternative. So deficient in every respect! Hideous in his person and without one good quality to make amends for it! His fortune to be sure is good. Yet not so very large! Three thousand a year. What is three thousand a year? It is but six times as much as my mother's income. It will not tempt me.'

'Yet it will be a noble fortune for Mary,' said Sophy, laughing again.

'For Mary! Yes indeed it will give me pleasure to see *her* in such affluence.'

Thus I ran on to the great entertainment of my sister till Mary came into the room to appearance in great agitation. She sat down. We made room for her at the fire. She seemed at a loss how to begin and at last said in some confusion. 'Pray, Sophy, have you any mind to be married?'

'To be married! None in the least. But why do you ask me? Are you acquainted with anyone who means to make me proposals?'

'I – no, how should I? But mayn't I ask a common question?'

'Not a very *common* one, Mary, surely,' said I.

She paused and after some moments' silence went on, 'How should you like to marry Mr Watts, Sophy?'

I winked at Sophy and replied for her. 'Who is there but must rejoice to marry a man of three thousand a year who keeps a post-chaise and pair, with silver harness, a boot before and a window to look out at behind?'

'Very true,' she replied, 'that's very true. So you would have him if he would offer, Georgiana? – and would *you*, Sophy?'

Sophy did not like the idea of telling a lie and deceiving her sister; she prevented the first and saved half her conscience by equivocation.

'I should certainly act just as Georgiana would do.'

'Well then,' said Mary, with triumph in her eyes, '*I* have had an offer from Mr Watts.'

We were, of course, very much surprised: 'Oh! do not accept him,' said I, 'and then perhaps he may have me.'

In short, my scheme took and Mary is resolved to do that to prevent our supposed happiness which she would not have done to ensure it in reality. Yet, after all, my heart cannot acquit me and Sophy is even more scrupulous. Quiet our minds, my dear Anne, by writing and telling us you approve our conduct. Consider it well over. Mary will have real pleasure in being a married woman, and able to chaperone us, which she certainly shall do, for I shall think myself bound to contribute as much as possible to her happiness in a state I have made her choose. They will probably have a new carriage, which will be paradise to her, and if we can prevail on Mr W. to set up his phaeton she will be too happy. These things, however, would be no consolation to Sophy or me for domestic misery. Remember all this and do not condemn us.

Friday

Last night, Mr Watts by appointment drank tea with us. As soon as his carriage stopped at the door, Mary went to the window.

'Would you believe it, Sophy,' said she, 'the old fool wants to have his new chaise just the colour of the old one, and hung as low too. But it shan't – I *will* carry my point. And if he won't let it be as high as the Duttons', and blue spotted with silver, I won't have him. Yes, I will too. Here he comes. I know he'll be rude; I know he'll be ill tempered and won't say one civil thing to me! nor behave at all like a lover.' She then sat down and Mr Watts entered.

'Ladies, your most obedient servant.'

We paid our compliments and he seated himself.

'Fine weather, ladies.' Then, turning to Mary, 'Well, Miss Stanhope, I hope you have *at last* settled the matter in your own mind, and will be so good as to let me know whether you will *condescend* to marry me or not.'

'I think, sir,' said Mary, 'you might have asked in

a genteeler way than that. I do not know whether I *shall* have you if you behave so odd.'

'Mary!' said my mother.

'Well, mama, if he will be so cross . . .'

'Hush, hush, Mary, you shall not be rude to Mr Watts.'

'Pray, madam, do not lay any restraint on Miss Stanhope by obliging her to be civil. If she does not choose to accept my hand, I can offer it elsewhere, for as I am by no means guided by a particular preference to you above your sisters, it is equally the same to me which I marry of the three.'

Was there ever such a wretch! Sophy reddened with anger and I felt *so* spiteful!

'Well then,' said Mary, in a peevish accent, 'I *will* have you if I *must*.'

'I should have thought, Miss Stanhope, that when such settlements are offered as I have offered to you there can be no great violence done to the inclinations in accepting of them.'

Mary mumbled out something, which I who sat close to her could just distinguish to be, 'What's the use of a great jointure if men live for ever?' And then audibly, 'Remember the pin money; two hundred a year.'

'A hundred and seventy-five, madam.'

'Two hundred indeed, sir,' said my mother.

'And remember I am to have a new carriage hung as high as the Duttons', and blue spotted with silver; and I shall expect a new saddle horse, a suit of fine lace, and an infinite number of the most valuable jewels. Diamonds such as never were seen, pearls as large as those of the Princess Badroulbadour in the fourth volume of *The Arabian Nights*, and rubies, emeralds, topazes, sapphires, amethysts, turkeystones, agate, beads, bugles and garnets, and pearls, rubies, emeralds and beads out of number. You must set up your phaeton, which must be cream-coloured, with a wreath of silver flowers round it, you must buy four of the finest bays in the kingdom and you must drive me in it every day. This is not all; you must entirely new furnish your house after my taste, you must hire two more footmen to attend me, two women to wait on me, must always let me do just as I please and make a very good husband.' Here she stopped, I believe rather out of breath.

'This is all very reasonable, Mr Watts, for my daughter to expect.'

'And it is very reasonable, Mrs Stanhope, that your daughter should be disappointed.' He was going on but Mary interrupted him.

'You must build me an elegant greenhouse and stock it with plants. You must let me spend every winter in Bath, every spring in town, every summer in taking some tour, and every autumn at a watering place, and if we are at home the rest of the year,' Sophy and I laughed, 'you must do nothing but give balls and masquerades. You must build a room on purpose and a theatre to act plays in. The first play we have shall be *Which is the Man*, and I will do Lady Bell Bloomer.'

'And pray, Miss Stanhope,' said Mr Watts, 'what am I to expect from you in return for all this?'

'Expect? why you may expect to have me pleased.'

'It would be odd if I did not. Your expectations, madam, are too high for me, and I must apply to Miss Sophy, who perhaps may not have raised hers so much.'

'You are mistaken, sir, in supposing so,' said Sophy, 'for though they may not be exactly in the same line, yet my expectations are to the full as high as my sister's; for I expect my husband to be good tempered and cheerful; to consult my happiness in all his actions, and to love me with constancy and sincerity.'

Mr Watts stared. 'These are very odd ideas truly, young lady. You had better discard them before you marry, or you will be obliged to do it afterwards.'

My mother in the meantime was lecturing Mary, who was sensible that she had gone too far, and when Mr Watts was just turning towards me in order, I believe, to address me, she spoke to him in a voice half-humble, half-sulky.

'You are mistaken, Mr Watts, if you think I was in earnest when I said I expected so much. However, I must have a new chaise.'

'Yes, sir, you must allow that Mary has a right to expect that.'

'Mrs Stanhope, I *mean* and have always meant to have a new one on my marriage. But it shall be the colour of my present one.'

'I think, Mr Watts, you should pay my girl the compliment of consulting her taste on such matters.'

Mr Watts would not agree to this, and for some time insisted upon its being a chocolate colour, while Mary was as eager for having it blue with silver spots. At length, however, Sophy proposed that to please Mr W. it should be a dark brown and to please Mary it should be hung rather high and have a silver border. This was at length agreed to, though reluctantly on both sides, as each had intended to carry their point entire. We then proceeded to other matters, and it was settled that they should be married as soon as the writings could be completed. Mary was very eager for a special licence and Mr Watts talked of banns. A common licence was at last agreed on. Mary is to have all the family jewels which are very inconsiderable, I believe, and Mr W. promises to buy her a saddle horse; but, in return, she is not to expect to go to town or any other public place for these three years. She is to have neither greenhouse, theatre or phaeton; to be contented with one maid without an additional footman. It engrossed the whole evening to settle these affairs; Mr W. supped with us and did not go till twelve. As soon as he was gone, Mary exclaimed, 'Thank heaven! he's off at last; how I do hate him!'

It was in vain that mama represented to her the impropriety she was guilty of in disliking him who was to be her husband, for she persisted in declaring her aversion to him and hoping she might never see him again. What a wedding will this be! Adieu, my dear Anne. Your faithfully sincere

GEORGIANA STANHOPE

4

The same to the same
Saturday
DEAR ANNE – Mary, eager to have everyone know of her approaching wedding and more particularly desirous of triumphing as she called it over the Duttons, desired us to walk with her this morning to Stoneham. As we had nothing else to do we readily agreed, and had as pleasant a walk as we could have with Mary, whose conversation entirely consisted in abusing the man she is so soon to marry and in longing for a blue chaise spotted with silver. When we reached the Duttons' we found the two girls in the dressing-room with a very handsome young man, who was of course introduced to us. He is the son of Sir Henry Brudenell of Leicestershire. Mr Brudenell is the handsomest man I ever saw in my life; we are all three very much pleased with him. Mary, who from the moment of our reaching the dressing-room had been swelling with the knowledge of her own importance and with the desire of making it known, could not remain long silent on the subject after we were seated, and soon addressing herself to Kitty said, 'Don't you think it will be necessary to have all the jewels new set?'

'Necessary for what?'

'For what! Why, for my appearance.'

'I beg your pardon, but I really do not understand you. What jewels do you speak of, and where is your appearance to be made?'

'At the next ball, to be sure, after I am married.'

You may imagine their surprise. They were at first incredulous, but on our joining in the story they at last believed it. 'And who is it to?' was of course the first question. Mary pretended bashfulness, and answered in confusion, her eyes cast down, 'To Mr Watts.' This also required confirmation from us, for that anyone who had the beauty and fortune (though small, yet a provision) of Mary would willingly marry Mr Watts could by them scarcely be credited. The subject being now fairly introduced and herself the object of everyone's attention in the company, she lost all her confusion and became perfectly unreserved and communicative.

'I wonder you should never have heard of it before, for in general things of this nature are very well known in the neighbourhood.'

'I assure you,' said Jemima, 'I never had the least suspicion of such an affair. Has it been in agitation long?'

'Oh, yes! ever since Wednesday.'

They all smiled, particularly Mr Brudenell.

'You must know Mr Watts is very much in love with me, so that it is quite a match of affection on his side.'

'Not on his only, I suppose,' said Kitty.

'Oh! when there is so much love on one side there is no occasion for it on the other. However, I do not much dislike him, though he is very plain to be sure.'

Mr Brudenell stared, the Miss Duttons laughed and Sophy and I were heartily ashamed of our sister.

She went on. 'We are to have a new post-chaise and very likely may set up our phaeton.'

This we knew to be false, but the poor girl was pleased at the idea of persuading the company that such a thing was to be and I would not deprive her of so harmless an enjoyment.

She continued. 'Mr Watts is to present me with the family jewels, which I fancy are very considerable.'

I could not help whispering to Sophy, 'I fancy not.'

'These jewels are what I suppose must be new set before they can be worn. I shall not wear them till the first ball I go to after my marriage. If Mrs Dutton should not go to it, I hope you will let me chaperone you; I shall certainly take Sophy and Georgiana.'

'You are very good,' said Kitty, 'and since you are inclined to undertake the care of young ladies, I should advise you to prevail on Mrs Edgecumbe to let you chaperone her six daughters, who with your two sisters and ourselves will make your entrée very respectable.'

Kitty made us all smile except Mary, who did not understand her meaning and coolly said that she should not like to chaperone so many. Sophy and I now endeavoured to change the conversation but succeeded only for a few minutes, for Mary took care to bring back their attention to her and her approaching wedding. I was sorry for my sister's sake to see that Mr Brudenell seemed to take pleasure in listening to her account of it and even encouraged her by his questions and remarks, for it was evident that his only aim was to laugh at her. I am afraid he found her very ridiculous. He kept his countenance extremely well, yet it was easy to see that it was with difficulty he kept it. At length, however, he seemed fatigued and disgusted with her ridiculous conversation, as he turned from her to us, and spoke but little to her for about half an hour before we left Stoneham. As soon as we were out of the house we all joined in praising the person and manners of Mr Brudenell.

We found Mr Watts at home.

'So, Miss Stanhope,' said he, 'you see I am come a-courting in a true lover-like manner.'

'Well, you need not have *told* me that. I knew why you came very well.'

Sophy and I then left the room, imagining, of course, that we must be in the way if a scene of courtship were to begin. We were surprised at being followed almost immediately by Mary.

'And is your courting so soon over?' said Sophy.

'Courting!' replied Mary, 'we have been quarrelling. Watts is such a fool! I hope I shall never see him again.'

'I am afraid you will,' said I, 'as he dines here today. But what has been your dispute?'

'Why, only because I told him that I had seen a man much handsomer than he was this morning he flew into a great passion and called me a vixen, so I only stayed to tell him I thought him a blackguard and came away.'

'Short and sweet,' said Sophy; 'but pray, Mary, how will this be made up?'

'He ought to ask my pardon; but if he did, I would not forgive him.'

'His submission then would not be very useful.'

When we were dressed we returned to the parlour where mama and Mr Watts were in close conversation. It seems that he had been complaining to her of her daughter's behaviour, and she had persuaded him to think no more of it. He therefore met Mary with all his accustomed civility, and, except one touch at the phaeton and another at the greenhouse, the evening went off with great harmony and cordiality. Watts is going to town to hasten the preparations for the wedding.

I am your affectionate friend,

G.S.

Evelyn

In a retired part of the county of Sussex there is a village (for what I know to the contrary) called Evelyn, perhaps one of the most beautiful spots in the south of England. A gentleman, passing through it on horseback about twenty years ago, was so entirely of my opinion in this respect that he put up at the little alehouse in it and enquired with great earnestness whether there were any house to be let in the parish.

The landlady, who as well as everyone else in Evelyn was remarkably amiable, shook her head at this question, but seemed unwilling to give him any answer. He could not bear this uncertainty – yet knew not how to obtain the information he desired. To repeat a question which had already appeared to make the good woman uneasy was impossible. He turned from her in visible agitation. 'What a situation am I in!' said he to himself as he walked to the window and threw up the sash. He found himself revived by the air, which he felt to a much greater degree when he had opened the window than he had done before. Yet it was but for a moment. The agonising pain of doubt and suspense again weighed down his spirits. The good woman who had watched in eager silence every turn of his countenance with that benevolence which characterises the inhabitants of

Evelyn, entreated him to tell her the cause of his uneasiness. 'Is there anything, sir, in my power to do that may relieve your griefs? Tell me in what manner I can soothe them and, believe me, the friendly balm of comfort and assistance shall not be wanting; for indeed, sir, I have a sympathetic soul.'

'Amiable woman,' said Mr Gower, affected almost to tears by this generous offer, 'this greatness of mind, in one to whom I am almost a stranger, serves but to make me the more warmly wish for a house in this sweet village. What would I not give to be your neighbour, to be blessed with your acquaintance and with the further knowledge of your virtues! Oh! with what pleasure would I form myself by such an example! Tell me then, best of women, is there no possibility? I cannot speak – you know my meaning –'

'Alas! sir,' replied Mrs Willis, 'there is *none*. Every house in this village, from the sweetness of the situation and the purity of the air, in which neither misery, ill health or vice are ever wafted, is inhabited. And yet,' after a short pause, 'there is a family, who though warmly attached to the spot, yet from a peculiar generosity of disposition would perhaps be willing to oblige you with their house.'

He eagerly caught at this idea, and having gained a direction to the place, he set off immediately on his walk to it. As he approached the house, he was delighted with its situation. It was in the exact centre of a small circular paddock, which was enclosed by a regular paling and bordered with a plantation of Lombardy poplars and spruce firs alternatively placed in three rows. A gravel walk ran through this beautiful shrubbery, and as the remainder of the paddock was unencumbered with any other timber, the surface of it perfectly even and smooth and grazed by four white cows, which were disposed at equal distances from each other, the whole appearance of the place as Mr Gower entered the paddock was uncommonly striking. A beautifully rounded, gravel road without any turn or interruption led immediately to the house.

Mr Gower rang – the door was soon opened. 'Are Mr and Mrs Webb at home?'

'My good sir, they are,' replied the servant; and leading the way, conducted Mr Gower upstairs into a very elegant dressing-room, where a lady, rising from her seat, welcomed him with all the generosity which Mrs Willis had attributed to the family.

'Welcome, best of men – welcome to this house, and to everything it contains. William, tell your master of the happiness I enjoy – invite him to partake of it. Bring up some chocolate immediately; spread a cloth in the dining-parlour and carry in the venison pasty. In the meantime, let the gentleman have some sandwiches, and bring in a basket of fruit – send up some ices and a basin of soup, and do not forget some jellies and cakes.' Then turning to Mr Gower, and taking out her purse, 'Accept this, my good sir – believe me you are welcome to everything that is in my power to bestow. I wish my purse were weightier, but Mr Webb must make up my deficiencies. I know he has cash in the house to the amount of a hundred pounds, which he shall bring you immediately.'

Mr Gower felt overpowered by her generosity as he put the purse in his pocket, and from the excess of his gratitude, could scarcely express himself intelligibly when he accepted her offer of the hundred pounds. Mr Webb soon entered the room, and repeated every protestation of friendship and cordiality which his lady had already made. The chocolate, the sandwiches, the jellies, the cakes, the ice and the soup soon made their appearance, and Mr Gower having tasted something of all, and pocketed the rest, was conducted into the dining-parlour, where he ate a most excellent dinner and partook of the most exquisite wines, while Mr and Mrs Webb stood by him still pressing him to eat and drink a little more.

'And now, my good sir,' said Mr Webb, when Mr Gower's repast was concluded, 'what else can we do to contribute to your happiness and express the affection we bear you. Tell us what you wish more to receive, and depend upon our gratitude for the communication of your wishes.'

'Give me then your house and grounds; I ask for nothing else.'

'They are yours,' exclaimed both at once; 'from this moment they are yours.' The agreement concluded on and the present accepted by Mr Gower, Mr Webb rang to have the carriage ordered, telling William at the same time to call the young ladies.

'Best of men,' said Mrs Webb, 'we will not long intrude upon your time.'

'Make no apologies, dear madam,' replied Mr Gower. 'You are welcome to stay this half-hour if you like it.'

They both burst forth into raptures of admiration at his politeness, which they agreed served only to make their conduct appear more inexcusable in trespassing on his time.

The young ladies soon entered the room. The elder of them was about seventeen, the other, several years younger. Mr Gower had no sooner fixed his eyes on Miss Webb than he felt that something more was necessary to his happiness than the house he had just received.

Mrs Webb introduced him to her daughter. 'Our dear friend Mr Gower, my love – he has been so good as to accept of this house, small as it is, and to promise to keep it for ever.'

'Give me leave to assure you, sir,' said Miss Webb, 'that I am highly sensible of your kindness in this respect, which from the shortness of my father's and mother's acquaintance with you, is more than usually flattering.'

Mr Gower bowed. 'You are too obliging, ma'am – I assure you that I like the house extremely – and if they would complete their generosity by giving me their elder daughter in marriage, with a handsome portion, I should have nothing more to wish for.'

This compliment brought a blush into the cheeks of the lovely Miss Webb, who seemed, however, to refer herself to her father and mother. *They* looked delighted at each other.

At length Mrs Webb, breaking silence, said, 'We bend under a weight of obligations to you which we can never repay. Take our girl, take our Maria, and on her must the difficult task fall of endeavouring to make some return to so much beneficence.'

Mr Webb added, 'Her fortune is but ten thousand pounds, which is almost too small a sum to be offered.'

This objection, however, being instantly removed by the generosity of Mr Gower, who declared himself satisfied with the sum mentioned, Mr and Mrs Webb, with their younger daughter, took their leave, and on the next day, the nuptials of their elder with Mr Gower were celebrated.

This amiable man now found himself perfectly happy: united to a very lovely and deserving young woman, with a handsome fortune and an elegant house, settled in the village of Evelyn and by that means enabled to cultivate his acquaintance with Mrs Willis. Could he have a wish ungratified? For some months he found that he could *not*, till one day, as he was walking in the shrubbery with Maria leaning on his arm, they observed a rose full-blown lying on the gravel; it had fallen from a rose tree which with three others had been planted by Mr Webb to give a pleasing variety to the walk. These four rose trees served also to mark the quarters of the shrubbery, by which means the traveller might always know how far in his progress round the paddock he was got.

Maria stooped to pick up the beautiful flower, and with all her family generosity presented it to her husband. 'My dear Frederic,' said she, 'pray take this charming rose.'

'Rose!' exclaimed Mr Gower. 'Oh, Maria! of what does not that remind me! Alas, my poor sister, how have I neglected you!'

The truth was that Mr Gower was the only son of a very large family, of which Miss Rose Gower was the thirteenth daughter. This young lady, whose merits deserved a better fate than she met with, was the darling of her relations. From the clearness of her skin and the brilliancy of her eyes, she was fully entitled to all their partial affection. Another circumstance contributed to the general love they bore her, and that was one of the finest heads of hair in the world. A few months before her brother's marriage, her heart had been engaged by the attentions and charms of a young man whose high rank and expectations seemed to foretell objections from his family to a match which would be highly desirable to theirs. Proposals were made on the young man's part, and proper objections on his father's – he was desired to return from Carlisle, where he was with his beloved Rose, to the family seat in Sussex. He was then obliged to comply, and the angry father then finding from his conversation how determined he was to marry no other woman, sent him for a fortnight to the Isle of Wight under the care of the family chaplain, with the hope of overcoming his constancy by time and absence in a foreign country. They accordingly prepared to bid a long adieu to England; the young nobleman was not allowed to see his Rose. They set sail but a storm arose which baffled the arts of the seamen. The vessel was wrecked on the coast of Calshot and every soul on board perished. The sad event soon reached Carlisle, and the beautiful Rose was affected by it beyond the power of expression. It was to soften her affliction by obtaining a picture of her unfortunate lover that her brother undertook a journey into Sussex, where he hoped that his petition would not be rejected by the severe yet afflicted father. When he reached Evelyn he was not many miles from — Castle, but the pleasing events which befell him in that place had for a while made him totally forget the object of his journey and his unhappy sister. The little incident of the rose, however, brought everything concerning her to his recollection again, and he bitterly repented his neglect. He returned to the house immediately, and agitated by grief, apprehension and shame, wrote the following letter to Rose.

July 14th, Evelyn

MY DEAREST SISTER – As it is now four months since I left Carlisle, during which period I have not once written to you, you will perhaps unjustly accuse me of neglect and forgetfulness. Alas! I blush when I own the truth of your accusation. Yet if you are still alive, do not think too harshly of me, or suppose that I could for a moment forget the situation of my Rose. Believe me, I will forget you no longer, but will hasten as soon as possible to — Castle if I find by your answer that you are still alive. Maria joins me in every dutiful and affectionate wish, and I am yours sincerely

F. GOWER

He waited in the most anxious expectation for an answer to his letter, which arrived as soon as the great distance from Carlisle would admit of. But, alas, it came not from Rosa.

Carlisle, July 17th

DEAR BROTHER – My mother has taken the liberty of opening your letter to poor Rose, as she has been dead these six weeks. Your long absence and continued silence gave us all great uneasiness and hastened her to the grave. Your journey to — Castle therefore may be spared. You do not tell us where you have been since the time of your quitting Carlisle, nor in any way account for your tedious absence, which gives us some surprise. We all unite in compliments to Maria, and beg to know who she is.

Your affectionate sister,
M. GOWER

This letter, by which Mr Gower was obliged to attribute to his own conduct his sister's death, was so violent a shock to his feelings that in spite of his living at Evelyn, where illness was scarcely ever heard of, he was attacked by a fit of the gout, which, confining him to his own room, afforded an opportunity to Maria of shining in that favourite character of Sir Charles Grandison's, a nurse. No woman could ever appear more amiable than Maria did under such circumstances, and at last by her unremitting attentions she had the pleasure of seeing him gradually recover the use of his feet. It was a blessing by no means lost on him, for he was no sooner in a condition to leave the house, than he mounted his horse, and rode to — Castle, wishing to find whether his lordship, softened by his son's death, might have been brought to consent to the match, had both he and Rose been alive. His amiable Maria followed him with her eyes till she could see him no longer, and then sinking into her chair, overwhelmed with grief, found that in his absence she could enjoy no comfort.

Mr Gower arrived late in the evening at the castle, which was situated on a woody eminence commanding a beautiful prospect of the sea. Mr Gower did not dislike the situation, though it was certainly greatly inferior to that of his own house. There was an irregularity in the fall of the ground, and a profusion of old timber which appeared to him ill suited to the style of the castle, for it being a building of a very ancient date, he thought it required the paddock of Evelyn Lodge to form a contrast, and enliven the structure. The gloomy appearance of the old castle, frowning on him as he followed its winding approach, struck him with terror. Nor did he think himself safe till he was introduced into the drawing-room where the family were assembled to tea. Mr Gower was a perfect stranger to everyone in the circle, but though he was always timid in the dark and easily terrified when alone, he did not want that more necessary and more noble courage which enabled him without a blush to enter a large party of superior rank, whom he had never seen before, and to take his seat among them with perfect indifference.

The name of Gower was not unknown to Lord — . He felt distressed and astonished, yet rose and received him with all the politeness of a well-bred man. Lady — , who felt a deeper sorrow at the loss of her son than his lordship's harder heart was capable of, could hardly keep her seat when she found that he was the brother of her lamented Henry's Rose.

'My lord,' said Mr Gower, as soon as he was seated, 'You are perhaps surprised at receiving a visit from a man whom you could not have the least expectation of seeing here. But my sister, my unfortunate sister, is the real cause of my thus troubling you. That luckless girl is now no more – and though *she* can receive no pleasure from the intelligence, yet for the satisfaction of her family I wish to know whether the death of this unhappy pair has made an impression on your heart sufficiently strong to obtain that consent to their marriage – which in happier circumstances you would not be persuaded to give – supposing that they now were both alive.'

His lordship seemed lost in astonishment. Lady — could not support the mention of her son, and left the room in tears; the rest of the family remained attentively listening, almost persuaded that Mr Gower was distracted. 'Mr Gower,' replied his lordship, 'this is a very odd question – it appears to me that you are supposing an impossibility. No one can more sincerely regret the death of my son than I have always done, and it gives me great concern to know that Miss Gower's was hastened by his. Yet to suppose them alive is destroying at once the motive for a change in my sentiments concerning the affair.'

'My lord,' replied Mr Gower in anger, 'I see that you are a most inflexible man, and that not even the death of your son can make you wish his future life happy. I will no longer detain your lordship. I see, I plainly see that you are a very vile man – and now I have the honour of wishing all your lordships and ladyships a good night.'

He immediately left the room, forgetting in the heat of his anger the lateness of the hour, which at any other time would have made him tremble, and leaving the whole company unanimous in their opinion of his being mad. When, however, he had mounted his horse and the great gates of the castle had shut him out, he felt a universal tremor throughout his whole frame. If we consider his situation, indeed – alone, on horseback, as late in the year as August and in the day as nine o'clock, with no light to direct him but that of the moon almost full, and the stars which alarmed him by their twinkling – who can refrain from pitying him? No house within a quarter of a mile, and a gloomy castle, blackened by the deep shade of walnuts and pines, behind him. He felt indeed almost distracted with his fears, and shutting his eyes till he arrived at the village, to prevent his seeing either gypsies or ghosts, he rode on a full gallop all the way.

On his return home, he rang the house-bell, but no one appeared, a second time he rang, but the door was not opened, a third and a fourth with as little success. Observing the dining-parlour window open, he leapt in and pursued his way through the house till he reached Maria's dressing-room, where he found all the servants assembled at tea. Surprised at so very unusual a sight, he fainted; on his recovery he found himself on the sofa, with his wife's maid kneeling by him, chafing his temples with Hungary water. From her he learned that his beloved Maria had been so much grieved at his departure that she had died of a broken heart about three hours after his departure.

He then became sufficiently composed to give the necessary orders for her funeral, which took place the Monday following, this being the Saturday. When Mr Gower had settled the order of the procession, he set out himself to Carlisle to give vent to his sorrow in the bosom of his family. He arrived there in high health and spirits, after a delightful journey of three days and a half. What was his surprise on entering the breakfast parlour to see Rose, his beloved Rose, seated on a sofa; at the sight of him she fainted, and would have fallen had not a gentleman, sitting with his back to the door, started up and saved her from sinking to the ground. She very soon came to herself and then introduced this gentleman to her brother as her husband, a Mr Davenport.

'But, my dearest Rose,' said the astonished Gower, 'I thought you were dead and buried.'

'Why, my dear Frederick,' replied Rose, 'I wished you to think so, hoping that you would spread the report about the country and it would thus by some means reach — Castle. By this I hoped somehow or other to touch the hearts of its inhabitants. It was not till the day before yesterday that I heard of the death of my beloved Henry, which I learned from Mr Davenport, who concluded by offering me his hand. I accepted it with transport, and was married yesterday.'

Mr Gower embraced his sister and shook hands with Mr Davenport; he then took a stroll into the town. As he passed by a public house, he called for a pot of beer, which was brought him immediately by his old friend Mrs Willis.

Great was his astonishment at seeing Mrs Willis in Carlisle. But not forgetful of the respect he owed her, he dropped on one knee, and received the frothy cup from her, more grateful to him than nectar. He instantly made her an offer of his hand and heart, which she graciously condescended to accept, telling him that she was only on a visit to her cousin, who kept the Anchor, and should be ready to return to Evelyn whenever he chose. The next morning they were married and immediately proceeded to Evelyn. When he reached home, he recollected that he had never written to Mr and Mrs Webb to inform them of the death of their daughter, which he rightly supposed they knew nothing of, as they never took in any newspapers. He immediately dispatched the following letter.

> *Evelyn. August 19th, 1809*
>
> DEAREST MADAM – How can words express the poignancy of my feelings! Our Maria, our beloved Maria, is no more; she breathed her last on Saturday the 12th of August. I see you now in an agony of grief, lamenting not your own, but my loss.

Rest satisfied, I am happy – possessed of my lovely Sarah, what more can I wish for?

Remain
Respectfully yours,
F. GOWER

Westgate Buildings, August 22nd

GENEROUS, BEST OF MEN – How truly we rejoice to hear of your present welfare and happiness! and how truly grateful are we for your unexampled generosity in writing to condole with us on the late unlucky accident which befell our Maria. I have enclosed a draught on our banker for £30, which Mr Webb joins with me in entreating you and the amiable Sarah to accept.

Your most grateful
ANNE AUGUSTA WEBB

Mr and Mrs Gower resided many years at Evelyn, enjoying perfect happiness, the just reward of their virtues. The only alteration which took place at Evelyn was that Mr and Mrs Davenport settled there in Mrs Willis's former abode and were for many years the proprietors of the White Horse Inn.

MACMILLAN COLLECTOR'S LIBRARY

All the books in this series:

A Carnival Jangle by Alice Dunbar Nelson

A Little Cloud by James Joyce

An Unwritten Novel by Virginia Woolf

The Home-Coming by Rabindranath Tagore

Jack and Alice by Jane Austen

The Curious Case of Benjamin Button by F. Scott Fitzgerald

The Daughters of the Late Colonel by Katherine Mansfield

The Murders in the Rue Morgue by Edgar Allan Poe

The Nightingale and the Rose by Oscar Wilde

The Speckled Band by Arthur Conan Doyle